Soulknit

Short Stories About PETS and Their PEOPLE

Varangi Vora

Second Edition, 2025

Paperback ISBN – 978-93-343-9794-9

Learn more on soulknit.com

Building a Kinder World

A note from the author

The animals in these pages found care, connection, and a place to belong. But many more remain unseen —resting by busy roads, facing hunger, rain, and being overlooked.

A share of the profits from the sale of each book will be donated to the Heads Up For Tails Foundation — a registered non-profit in India focused on community animal welfare.

Through feeding drives, water-bowl initiatives, shelter support, adoption, and rescue work, the HUFT Foundation is helping build a kinder world for street animals.

By buying this book, you become a part of this world of kindness. Thank you for seeing value in every life.

You can read more about this initiative at soulknit.com.

For Piper, My Beloved Cat

In the stillness of the night, as I embraced the rhythms of motherhood, you stayed by my side—steadfast, patient, and kind. During these quiet moments, with your gentle presence, these stories came to life.

"Until one has loved an animal, a part of one's soul remains unawakened."

– Anatole France

"Until one has loved an animal, a part of one's soul remains unawakened."

– Anatole France

Contents

Preface 1

The Inheritance 3

A New Lease on Love 9

The Healing Purrs 15

The Sleep Remedy 21

For the Love of Idli 26

The Pandemic Paws 34

Of Fur and Memory 43

Acknowledgements 47

About the Author 52

Preface

I did not plan to write this book. The stories came through me. Just like I did not plan to have pets. They just came to me.

When I became a new mother, life shifted in ways I could never have fully prepared for. The exhaustion was deep, but so was the love—fierce, consuming, and unlike anything I ever experienced. Through the sleepless nights of feeding, burping, rocking, shushing, and pacifying, my cat Piper remained a quiet, steady presence. Watchful, affectionate, and patient.

Though she had only been with me for about a year before I got pregnant, it felt as though she had always been there, woven into the rhythms of my life. Piper is not a cat of many sounds, but she says a lot. She brushes past me with a quick tap on my leg when she wants to play, her tail all fluffed up. When her bowl is empty, she simply sits beside it, glancing between me and the untouched space, making her request without a single meow. As I fill my water bottle in the kitchen, she waits patiently by the door, knowing fresh water will come her way. She never clamors for attention, yet she always makes herself known. She never speaks, yet she is impossible to ignore.

Our family dog, Cooper, visited often around this time, adding to the vibrant dynamic of our home. While his stay was temporary, he brought joy and companionship to our growing family.

Together, Piper and Cooper showed me the profound ways pets weave themselves into our lives, offering comfort, love, and moments of unexpected adventure. These stories are a reflection of those moments—the tender connections, the unspoken understanding, and the adventures shared with the pets who weave themselves into the fabric of our lives.

Thank you for joining me in celebrating these bonds.

The Inheritance

"You have to take care of Biscuit," she said faintly. He watched as his mother separated the carrots from her pulao. She was in a hospital bed, battling the last days of her life and, as usual, also battling the carrots.

They were discussing her will and possessions. She was an exceptionally organized woman whose meticulous nature had ensured her affairs were in order long before she became ill. However, one unresolved matter lingered—the fate of her beloved cat. Biscuit was a relatively new addition to his mother's life but, had become dear to her.

His mother had always been fiercely independent, but after his father passed away, that fierce independence faltered. The grief had hit her harder than Vinay had anticipated; they had been together for 55 years.

During those dark months, a friend had gifted her a kitten. The tiny creature—no bigger than a teacup—had pulled his mother out of her shell. Biscuit became the focus of her care, and in turn, she found purpose again. She began sending him pictures and videos of Biscuit's antics—climbing curtains, chasing shadows—daily, even though Vinay visited regularly. The cat had become her lifeline.

"Biscuit will keep you grounded," she said, bringing him back to the present. Her eyes twinkled. "Maybe he'll stop you from bouncing between relationships."

"Ouch, Mom," Vinay said with a smile. Though her tone was teasing, he knew her well; she was worried about him. The monitors beeped rhythmically, filling the room's silence.

His mother was not wrong about him. He couldn't bear the pain and loneliness of heartbreak. His recent past had been marked by many short-lived relationships, but he had no idea how a cat would change that. However, this was his mother's last wish.

He swallowed the lump in his throat and nodded. "I'll take care of Biscuit."

"Thank you. You'll love living with Biscuit. You'll see," she said, her eyes welling with tears.

Vinay hugged her tightly, his heart heavy. He would miss her more than he could bear.

When his mother passed away, it hit him. He was all alone in this world. He'd known this was coming, but he did not foresee the vacuum that would engulf him after her death. A force field of love that had always surrounded him suddenly diminished. Would anyone else love him as she had?

True to his word, he brought Biscuit home. The cat kept to himself, slinking around the apartment as though still waiting for his mother to return. Vinay tried his best—feeding him, changing his litter—but there was an emptiness between them. Both man and cat were grieving in their own way.

Vinay threw himself into sorting through his mother's things. Each item was a prop from her life: a shawl that smelled like her, pieces of antique jewelry, photos capturing moments frozen in time. These were his inheritance, objects laden with memories, reminders of a life well-lived.

After taking care of her last belongings, he realized he hadn't seen Biscuit in a while. Panic rose inside him as he called for the cat. His calls went unanswered, as they always did.

Vinay retraced his steps in a flurry. Had Biscuit escaped when he'd opened the garage? He searched frantically, the panic growing with each passing second. He couldn't lose his last living connection to his mother.

Finally, he opened the cupboard where he had stored his mother's shawl. There, nestled in the soft fabric, was Biscuit.

Seeing the cat asleep in his mother's shawl broke something inside Vinay. He sank to the floor, relief flooding through him as tears poured down his face. He hugged Biscuit and the shawl together, feeling his mother's presence in that quiet, heart-wrenching moment.

Biscuit stayed still, accepting Vinay's touch for the first time without retreating or batting him away. Something shifted between them.

Later, Vinay placed Biscuit on the couch with the shawl and scrolled through his phone, watching old videos of his mother playing with Biscuit.

The cat's ears perked up as soon as her voice came through the speaker. Biscuit inched closer to the phone, nuzzling it gently. A fresh wave of emotion crashed over Vinay. He wasn't truly alone. His mother had made sure of that. The day had been emotionally exhausting, but there was a tender, healing quality to it as well.

Vinay forgot to order Biscuit's usual food, so he improvised. Biscuit sniffed the new food skeptically, letting out a displeased meow before eventually digging in.

When Vinay checked later, he noticed tiny pieces of orange left in the bowl. He leaned in to get a better look and laughed out loud. The leftover pieces were carrots.

Even now, his mother's spirit seemed to linger—her battle with carrots had passed on to the cat. Her love was still present, a force-field that could never disappear.

Vinay sat back on the couch, Biscuit climbing into his lap, something he'd never done before. Stroking the cat, Vinay felt an unfamiliar sense of peace. Their new normal was settling in, one purr at a time.

A New Lease on Love

Although Vikram and his wife Sonal had no children, he sometimes felt he was already parenting—his mother. This was one of those moments. His mother looked at him, expectation etched deeply on her face. Vikram's love for her and the growing responsibility of caring for her pushed against good reason. He could already picture his wife Sonal giving him a knowing smile. He sighed, rubbing his temple, and said, "Fine."

At 65, Vikram's mother wanted to bring home a dog. She was understandably lonely since his father had passed away. Vikram and Sonal worked long hours as IT professionals; his mother was usually home alone.

Nevertheless, they couldn't imagine caring for a dog, especially since his mother had bad knees and couldn't walk well. "I'll take him out and get some exercise myself," she had told Vikram.

In Vikram's experience, nothing encouraged his mother to walk regularly. There was always an excuse not to go. But he loved his mother dearly, and he was determined to fulfill her wishes after his father's passing.

The night before, he had confidently told Sonal, "This time, I'm putting my foot down." She'd laughed, poked him in the ribs, and said, "You'll give in. You love her too much."

As usual, she was right. Max, their adopted pup, arrived in the family with boundless energy. Vikram's mother chose the name Max because it was short for Maximilian, meaning "the greatest."

From the moment he set his paw in their home, it was clear that he would change everything. For the better or for the worse, the verdict was still out.

But change, as it often is, was chaotic. Vikram wrinkled his nose as he stepped into the living room, the unmistakable scent of puppy accidents lingering in the air. That was the price they paid for adopting a pup. He was adorable, but that cuteness came at a cost.

Max was a spirited pup. His excitement levels were always off the charts. His answer to everything was a HELL YES, and channeling this energy drained Sonal and Vikram.

After several nights of barking, sleeplessness, and cleaning up messes, Sonal had had enough. She hunched over her laptop, searching desperately for a solution. Dog training videos filled the screen, emphasizing the need for a dependable schedule and a primary person to handle the training.

The following day, Sonal sat at the kitchen table with Vikram's mother. "I found some training videos," Sonal told her. "They say we need one person to lead the training. Would you be willing to try?"

Vikram's mother raised her eyebrows and glanced at the pup, who was happily chewing on a bone. "Bringing a dog into our lives was my decision," she said slowly. "I'll do my part."

Max's training commenced the next day. Armed with knowledge from several videos, Vikram's mother embraced the daily routine. Vikram and Sonal supported her, but it was clear that she was Max's center of attention.

One evening, as Sonal collapsed on the couch after hours of video calls, Max trotted over and lay his head in her lap.

"We are all done for the day," Vikram said, joining her.

"We're getting there," she said softly, scratching the pup's chin. "We are learning each other's language."

"Which language is that?"

Sonal smiled. "The language of love."

Even though Max was still rough around the edges, the house began to settle into a new rhythm. Sonal and Vikram adjusted their schedules to give the pup time and attention, and Vikram's mother found joy in her newfound role. The daily exercise strengthened her knees and filled her heart.

One day, Sonal watched as Vikram's mother played ball with Max outside. Both were basking in the sun's golden glow, spent but happy. "Look at them," she said, waving Vikram over.

He joined her, wrapping his arm around her waist. "It's been a long time since I've seen her like this," he said, his voice low. "So active. So... happy."

Vikram's mother came inside, cheeks flushed from the cool evening air, Max trotting faithfully behind her. She sat beside them in the living room, resting her hand gently on Max's head.

"Thank you for this," she said, her voice full of emotion. "He's brought so much love."

The binary forces in the house—order and chaos, youth and age, independence and dependence—had found a strange harmony.

Max rested his wet nose on Vikram's feet, panting softly, and Vikram bent down to scratch him behind the ears. Unexpectedly, he'd grown fond of Max, too.

They had thought there was no time for a pet in their family, but now they were complete in a way they had never imagined. Bringing Max into their lives had given them all a new lease on love.

The Healing Purrs

When Tara brought Mika home, she imagined a playful pet she could cuddle with, record funny videos, and spend hours playing with. She thought Mika would at least respond when called. But she quickly learned she had adopted a cat, not a pet, and there was a significant difference between the two.

Tara adopted Mika from a local shelter. She had no mother and was the only survivor from her litter. Tara hoped she would fill her loneliness when Kabir, her husband, traveled for work.

However, Mika kept her distance, avoiding cuddles and only allowing herself to be petted when she felt like it. Kabir warned Tara that Mika probably had past trauma and that building trust would take time.

Logically, Tara understood, but her heart ached at Mika's coldness. The quiet house, the empty nursery, and the kitten's aloofness revived old feelings of inadequacy that Tara thought she had buried long ago.

One day, Kabir brought Mika some melty treats, the kind you feed directly from the wrapper. The pet store owner claimed they were irresistible. Kabir thought they might help melt the icy barrier between Mika and Tara, but Mika only glanced at the treat with disdain.

With a sigh, Tara placed the open treat on the windowsill and busied herself with dinner. It wasn't until an hour later that she heard a small bleat. She looked up, and Mika was sniffing the treat, making tiny, tentative sounds and glancing toward Tara.

For the first time, Tara felt a connection. She turned off the stove and fed Mika the treat. Encouraged, she began feeding her treats every day. Kabir stocked up on dozens of packs, enjoying the spark of joy in Tara's eyes each time Mika ate from her hands.

But despite the treats, Mika kept to herself, never allowing Tara to get too close. She had become accustomed to living alone, even with company in the house. Then, one day, everything changed.

Tara and Kabir came home from the hospital, devastated. Their pregnancy had ended too soon. Tara had miscarried just days after conceiving. She curled up on the sofa, binge-watching old TV shows, unable to face the emptiness within her. Kabir tried to comfort her, but she was unreachable. So he stayed with her, watching over her and waking up in the middle of the night to check on her.

One evening, as Kabir returned from grocery shopping, he noticed that Mika had moved over to the corner of the couch. Assuming that she wanted Tara to give her a treat (they'd forgotten all about it), he handed Tara a treat.

Tara took it with little interest and fed it to Mika. Even after the treat was finished, Mika did not move. She stretched, licked herself clean, and stayed on the couch in her corner. Tara sighed and plopped back on her mountain of pillows.

Then, as Tara picked up the TV remote, Mika walked confidently over to Tara and curled into a little ball on her chest. Tara and Kabir looked at each other, unsure of Mika's plan. Mika sniffed Tara for a while, rested her head on her paws, and slept as if it was the most natural thing to do. As if she did that every day.

A small smile formed on Tara's lips. She looked at Kabir and whispered, "She is purring on my heart."

Kabir smiled and gently suggested, "Why don't you nap with her?"

Tara hesitated, then nodded and closed her eyes. She was exhausted from all the emotions. As Mika's body gently vibrated with her purrs, Tara felt secure, safe, and accepted as she was. She let go of her insecurities and gave in to the heartwarming moment—to Mika's soothing purrs.

The kitten was saying so much without saying anything at all.

Tara put her arms around Mika, and she cried. As her tears flowed, Mika snuggled closer, sharing in the pain. Tara had lost her unborn child. Mika had lost her mother at birth. They were destined to be together, sharing a bond only a mother and a child would know.

Kabir silently put away the groceries but kept his misty eyes on Tara and Mika. After Googling cat purrs and being convinced that it was safe for Tara, he went to bed.

Kabir awoke to the familiar smell of freshly brewed coffee the following day. Tara had returned to the kitchen—her usual self—and handed him a cup just as he liked it. He smiled, grateful to see her smile again. He started making breakfast, savoring the signs of healing.

Tara cuddled in Kabir's arms that night, and Mika snoozed at their feet. Tara whispered to him, "I think Mika healed me. Her hugs and purrs made me whole again. I'm okay. I'm sorry I wasn't there for you earlier, but I am here now. We will get through this together."

Kabir was glad to have her back. He hugged her a little tighter, and they continued talking in hushed tones for hours.

Two months later, Tara was pregnant again. This time, Mika never left her side. For the next nine months, the bond between Tara and Mika grew stronger, as if Mika instinctively knew that her comforting presence was still needed. Mika became Tara's constant companion, and when the baby finally arrived, it was clear that Mika's place in their family was as permanent as any heartbeat.

The Sleep Remedy

Arjun and Priya loved mornings. Their routine was sacred—an early start, a quiet cup of coffee together, and the joy of watching their 7-year-old daughter, Sara, running down the stairs with an excited squeal at 7:30 AM. "Good morning, Mommy and Daddy!" she would announce, bright-eyed and well-rested. Sara had always been a good sleeper like her parents and thrived on routine.

But ever since they'd moved into the new house, their peaceful mornings had become a distant memory. Sara could no longer sleep at night.

The decision to move had been easy. Priya was offered a promotion and needed to travel to the company headquarters often. Since Arjun's job was remote, he insisted they move so she could spend less time traveling. The move also meant they would be in a better neighborhood and closer to several good schools.

On paper, everything was perfect. But Sara struggled to fit in, and no matter what they tried, nothing seemed to help her sleep through the night. Arjun and Priya tried everything they could think of.

The decision to buy an aquarium was born out of desperation. A sleep therapist had suggested it, claiming that the gentle, rhythmic movements of the fish might help lull Sara into a peaceful slumber.

"It's likely a phase as she adjusts," the doctor reassured them. "She misses her old friends."

Still, it had been six weeks, and Sara's sleepless nights had exhausted the family. Arjun often woke up in the middle of the night, scrunched beside Sara—awake, tired, and yawning but unable to sleep.

Arjun looked at Sara, her chin resting on her folded hands next to the aquarium as she watched the fish flitter. The water tank magnified the dark circles under her exhausted eyes. Guilt settled like a heavy weight on his chest.

When Priya had asked if she would like a fish tank in her room, Sara had responded with maturity beyond her years. "I don't know, Mom, but I am open to trying," she said.

Arjun and Priya were researchers. They read everything about owning an aquarium and watched videos so Sara could also participate in the process. They selected a freshwater aquarium, considering its ease of maintenance. They also chose vibrant fish and decor. According to a video they watched together, colorful aquariums were more calming.

With the aquarium set up and the fish settled in, Sara observed it with curiosity and hope. "Dad, it's beautiful. I like it," she exclaimed.

Arjun couldn't help but mirror her smile. Hopefully, this new addition would solve her sleep challenge.
Later that day, they fed the fish little food pellets as the pet shop owner had recommended. They still needed to figure out how the new lights worked, but

Arjun was able to put a small LED light just above the aquarium. His daughter was right; it looked beautiful.

"Are you sure you don't want me to sleep with you tonight?" Arjun asked.

Sara shook her head. "I'll be okay, Daddy. If I need you, I'll knock."

Before going to bed, Arjun peeked into Sara's room. Her face reflected the light's soft glow as she stared at the aquarium, snuggling in her favorite blue blanket.

"She is awake but enchanted by the aquarium," he told Priya as he slid into bed beside her.

"You have to give her some time," Priya said, touching his shoulder.

He agreed, and before he knew it, the sleepless nights beside Sara caught up to him. He was fast asleep within minutes of hitting his pillow.

In the days that followed, the aquarium worked its magic. Slowly but surely, Sara's sleep improved. Every fish in the tank had a name and their own personality. Sara even began talking about new friends at school.

It was a warm summer morning, and Arjun and Priya were catching up over coffee when they heard it —the music of their daughter's feet pattering down the stairs. Arjun looked at Priya, a smile spreading across his face as Sara entered the kitchen, beaming.

"Good morning, Mommy and Daddy!" she chirped, the tiredness in her eyes replaced with energy.

Arjun beamed from ear to ear. He set his coffee cup down and began making breakfast.

"I love my fishies. Thank you so much!" Sara declared as Priya kissed her forehead.

Arjun and Priya had made many important decisions that had changed their lives in big ways—a new job, better school, etc.- but ultimately, the small things brought them the most joy: a little aquarium, a few colorful fish, and a simple solution to a problem that had seemed insurmountable.

Sara's laughter echoed through the kitchen as they sat down to breakfast, and at that moment, Arjun knew they had made the right choices—big and small.

For the Love of Idli

She came uncomfortably close to him, touching her wet nose all over his white pajamas and wagging her tail. Narenji was sitting at his usual table at the South Indian restaurant he frequented.

"Shoo!" he whispered, and turned away from her.

The dog merely sat at his feet expectantly, her tongue hanging from her mouth.

Saliva dripped on Narenji's toe. He flinched and scooted away from her.

His memories of living with his son and daughter-in-law were still raw. They'd brought home a puppy, and he couldn't stand it. The licking, the smell, the poop and pee everywhere—it had been too much for him. It had taken him a month to realize they would not return the puppy.

Narenji had tried everything, short of a hunger strike. They'd remained unfazed, respectful, and annoyingly happy with the needy puppy. He had moved out the following month despite their insistence on staying.

An apartment on the same floor was on the market for rent, and he promptly signed the lease. "How bad can it be?" he'd thought before moving. His son and daughter-in-law were at work all day, and he was home alone anyway. At least he wouldn't have to deal with the dog.

He never thought he'd miss the things he never noticed: the smell of his daughter-in-law's coffee in the morning, the voice of his son chanting the Ganpati mantra, the way groceries just appeared on time, their soft and sweet banter. These small things filled their home with warmth.

Last night had been particularly difficult. He sat on his new balcony listening to old Hindi songs. The sharp sting of broken relationships had deepened as the songs changed from love to love lost and pain. The aroma of jasmine flowers from the balcony below had mingled with his thoughts, adding to the bittersweet nostalgia. He hadn't known what ached more, his leg or his heart.

He grunted as he stirred from his thoughts and looked down at the dog sitting next to him at the restaurant.

Jitu, the owner of the Taste of Chennai, looked up from behind the billing counter and noticed the exchange. He had known Narenji for years—a regular customer who lived in the building across the street. Every Sunday at 11:00 AM, Narenji ordered three Idlis, a vada, extra coconut chutney, and filter coffee. A man of routine, Narenji wore a perpetual scowl and always twiddled his cane as if it were a shield from the world.

Jitu knew more than most about Narenji's history. His son had confided in him after Narenji's stroke and the pain in his leg. Since the death of his wife, Narenji had become a shadow of the man he used to be. But his weekly visits to Taste of Chennai remained constant, even if everything else in his life felt unmoored.

Jitu whistled and signaled for the dog—Kokum—to stay away. Kokum took a few steps back and curled into a ball on the floor, panting and drooling. While Jitu knew Kokum was harmless, he did not want to upset Narenji. It was clear that she wanted to eat Idli.

Kokum had wandered into his establishment a few days ago. Her collar, gentle demeanor, and well-maintained mane indicated she was someone's pet and most likely lost. Jitu took care of her, hoping her owner would show up soon, but he was losing hope with each passing day.

When Narenji finished his meal, he hobbled to his feet, cane tapping on the sidewalk as he walked home. He didn't notice Kokum quietly trailing behind him.

"Kokum! Come here!" Jitu called when she did not respond to his whistles. She looked back and hesitated, then continued walking behind Narenji.

They disappeared as they turned into the lane leading to the society gate. Jitu was momentarily distracted as more customers streamed in. When he looked up after the afternoon rush was over, he noticed Kokum sitting in her usual spot under the tree.

As the weeks passed, Kokum's strange behavior persisted. Every Sunday, she accompanied Narenji from his home to the restaurant and back again. She sat at his feet while he ate, always with that same look of quiet expectation. Narenji was annoyed at first but gradually grew accustomed to her presence. Still, he refused to acknowledge her.

After a few weeks, Narenji noticed Kokum following him. "Lord Ganesha is playing a cruel trick on me!" he exclaimed. "My only companion is the creature that plunged me into this lonesome state."

To his son and daughter-in-law's credit, they visited him several times to check in on him and fill his kitchen with things he liked. While this would have been a great arrangement when his wife was alive, now he missed the hustle and bustle of their home.

One afternoon, Jitu placed an extra plate of Idlis on the table. "For her," he said, gesturing toward Kokum.

Narenji waved it off but hesitated as he stood up to leave. He picked up the plate, looked down at Kokum, and asked aloud, "Is this what you want?"

Kokum sniffed the Idlis, then gently nibbled them from his hand. Narenji watched in quiet disbelief, letting the Idli fall from his grasp. For the first time in months, he felt something soften inside him.

He wiped his hands on the edge of his shawl and started walking home in a huff. Kokum dutifully followed, after chomping down the Idlis. When Narenji realized that Kokum was still walking with him, he groaned. "What do you want? Why are you still following me?!"

Exasperated, he continued walking.

Kokum continued escorting him to and from the Taste of Chennai every Sunday. And from that day on, Narenji grudgingly ordered an extra plate of Idlis for her.

Then, one morning, Kokum came barking frantically to Jitu. She darted between the restaurant and the road. Alarmed, Jitu followed her and found Narenji collapsed on the sidewalk, convulsing. Jitu rushed to his side, loosening his kurta, turning him to the side, and calling for an ambulance. He called Narenji's son and reassured him, "Help is on the way."

He gently stroked Kokum's head, murmuring, "She came running for you, Narenji. She may have just saved your life."

A few days later, when Narenji was back home from the hospital, he woke up to loud panting and a slimy, wet touch. He looked at his hand and saw Kokum.

He looked up at his daughter-in-law, smiling.

"We bathed her and got her vaccinated," she said. "She's been waiting for you."

Narenji chuckled, rubbing Kokum's head. "Thank you, dear," he muttered, a smile tugging at his lips.

For the first time, the house didn't feel so empty.

A few weeks later, Narenji sat on the balcony, an upbeat tune playing in the background as his daughter-in-law shuffled a deck of cards. His son handed him a glass of lemonade while Narenji studied the cards in his hand.

Kokum lay peacefully at his feet, her nose resting on his slipper, while the pup gnawed happily on a bone under the table.

The cards in his hand were dreadful, but Narenji smiled. He had been dealt a good hand in life after all —one filled with unexpected companionship and joy, accepting that not one but two dogs were destined to share his life.

Every Sunday, Kokum accompanied Narenji to the Taste of Chennai to indulge in a plate of Idlis—the very food that had forged an unbreakable bond between them.

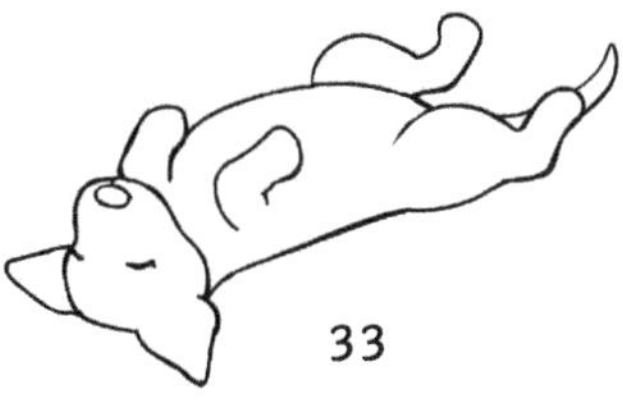

The Pandemic Paws

Jimmy's feet were cold, and he had forgotten to wear his socks again. He was too exhausted to get them and too cold to sleep. He curled tighter in the blanket, but it wasn't enough. The cold nipped at his toes and intensified the tightness in his chest. A restlessness building on his anxiety was taking hold.

The world had stopped 38 days ago. The government had declared a lockdown due to the COVID-19 pandemic, and it was uncertain when the lockdown would end.

Jimmy was an engineer. He managed a team that designed and manufactured electric circuit breakers and fuse boxes. He was one of the youngest engineers, but since his job wasn't classified as "essential," so he was working from home. Alone.

When the lockdown first happened, he had embraced it, seeing it as an opportunity to catch up on his task list. But as the days blended, he began questioning his solitary living situation.

Jimmy lived in his uncle's bungalow in the Serenade Villas Society. His uncle lived in the USA and needed someone to care for the house. Jimmy did it in exchange for rent-free living.

But after the lockdown, he began to hear the house's emptiness—the soft creaks of the doors, the refrigerator's hum, the fan's whirring. As the clock ticked in his room, the silence weighed on him.

The following day, Jimmy sat by the window, gripping his hot coffee cup with his cold hands. He glanced outside the window, and movement across the street caught his eye. His neighbor threaded a big box labeled "Donation" through the front door. She placed the box on the porch and picked up something beside it.

It was a white calico cat. His neighbor lingered for a moment, fingers brushing the cat's collar. She unclasped the collar and pocketed it. With her shoulders stiffened, she said something to the cat that Jimmy could not hear. Then she went back inside and shut the door.

Jimmy placed his coffee on the table and leaned closer to the window. "Was this... deliberate?" he wondered. The cat scratched its now-empty neck with its leg and curled up on the box.

That night, after switching off the light, Jimmy lingered by the window, scanning the neighbor's porch. The street was quiet, and nothing stirred, but there she was—the calico, sitting as still as a statue, her unblinking gaze fixed on the closed door of the house that had once been hers. Something tightened in Jimmy's chest, but he shook it off and shut the curtains.

When he opened the curtains the next day, the cat was still there, her fur puffed up. He made his coffee and sat by the window, keeping the cat company.

In India, stray animals were common. Dogs, cats, and cows roamed the streets, often unnoticed, blending into the background of daily life. People were focused on survival, and animal welfare rarely made the list of priorities. Jimmy never gave much thought to the animals around him. Still, he was transfixed by this cat—its dire situation and loneliness.

Then, as abruptly as the world had shut down, it opened again. Jimmy was called back to work. He was dressed and ready to leave. As he sipped his coffee that morning, he noticed a moving truck parked across the street. He frowned, scanning the porch and garden for the cat. It was nowhere in sight. "I'll check later," he muttered. But his first day back to work was busier than he imagined. He loved meeting everyone in person. He got back home exhausted and forgot all about the cat.

The following day, Jimmy woke with a fever and a sore throat. His company told him to stay home for two weeks, again. The frustration settled heavily on him. Another stretch of isolation.

Another lonely morning. He made his coffee and sat by the window. The moving truck from the day before pulled out of the parking, filled to the brim with boxes. Jimmy's eyes flicked back and forth, searching for any sign of the cat.

Then, as the neighbors got into their car to leave, the cat darted out from behind the gate. Fast as a flash, it leaped into the backseat.

The woman screamed, startled, then shoved the cat back onto the driveway. The door slammed, and the car pulled away without a second glance.

The cat stayed where she'd landed, crouched at the edge of the gate, her eyes fixed on the shrinking car until long after the taillights disappeared.

Just like the cat, Jimmy couldn't believe it. Something inside him cracked open. He sank into his chair and let his hands hold his heavy head. The tears came slowly at first, then surging, carrying with them months of pent-up fear, loneliness, and unexplained anger.

He'd told himself that being alone didn't bother him, that the loneliness was manageable. But now, watching the cat huddle alone in the growing dark, that lie unraveled, leaving him raw and exposed.

When he finally pulled himself together, it was evening. He made a simple dinner and sat down with a pen and paper. There were only two things he could think of doing:

- Order cat food
- Talk to a psychologist

Satisfied with these small steps, he slept soundly for the first time in weeks.

The next day, he woke up without a fever and followed his plan. He ordered the cat food and scheduled an appointment with a psychologist online.

The conversation with the psychologist went well—better than expected—but the cat was another matter. It was still holed up on the porch of the empty house, waiting for its owners to return. The messages in the Serenade Villas WhatsApp group confirmed what Jimmy already suspected—they had moved out.

He approached the cat, but it hissed and backed away when he tried to pet it. Undeterred, he left the food on the porch and observed it from afar.

Over the next few days, Jimmy learned more about cats online, joined a Cat Chat Therapy group, and spent hours chatting with fellow cat owners. He discovered that the cat was female. He named her Luna, a bright moon in the darkest night.

Like millions of cat lovers, Jimmy was hooked. He learned that cats were mysterious creatures—warm yet ferocious, agile yet affectionate. Their claws could hurt, but their purrs could heal. Revered for their independence and grace, they embodied a blend of irony and unpredictability that felt oddly therapeutic.

It took weeks before Luna let him touch her, but their bond grew steadily. Jimmy's spirits lifted, and he started making small changes. When his quarantine ended, he returned to work, but Luna was never far from his thoughts.

One evening, he came home to find her waiting on his porch. She had never done that before. He approached her slowly and noticed she was limping. Her paw was bleeding.

Carefully, he removed his jacket, wrapped it around her, and lifted her into his car, his heart pounding with concern and love for this little furry creature.

Though the vet's office was about to close, he took Luna in, and the vet treated the wound. "She's healthy otherwise," the vet told him. "The paw will heal in a few weeks."

Relieved, Jimmy wrapped her back into his jacket and drove her home.

Soon, another lockdown was announced, but it didn't affect Jimmy the same way. Luna had been living with him for a few weeks, and her paw had healed. She filled the house with energy and mischief. His laptop became her "cattop," often adorned with her sprawled-out body, making work an amusing challenge.

Her favorite hideout was the cupboard, where she peeked out with mischievous eyes, ready to pounce. She left trails of unrolled toilet paper like streamers and batted at his shoelaces whenever he tied them. During video calls, she'd stroll across the screen, to the surprise of his colleagues.

Jimmy caught himself smiling in the mirror. For the first time in months, the house no longer felt empty. While she was quiet, signs of Luna were everywhere.

"It's weird," Jimmy told his therapist during his session. "I thought I was losing my mind that day, but Luna showed up. Maybe I needed her more than she needed me."

As Jimmy slid under the blanket that night, he realized his feet were cold again. He rubbed them together half-heartedly, too tired to fetch his socks.

Just as he began to drift off, Luna slipped beneath the covers, curling herself over his toes like a tiny, purring heater. Her soft fur warmed him in seconds, but the warmth spread further than his legs. Jimmy smiled, pulling the blanket tighter around them.

The world outside could stay closed for all he cared. Right here, with Luna, was enough.

Of Fur and Memory

If you've ever wiped your tears on fur, whispered secrets to a tail-wagger, or been healed by a heartbeat that isn't your own—these pages are for you.

Write your Soulknit story here.

Of Fur and Memory

A space to let your heart write of the pet who shaped your days in quiet, beautiful ways.

We'd love to read your story at book@soulknit.com and see your pet photos @soulknit.stories on Instagram and Threads.

Acknowledgements

To my parents, Prathibha and Deepak Vora—thank you for giving me the space to be wholly myself. When I became a mother, your care only deepened. You welcomed Avi, Piper, and me for over ten months with such tenderness, making room for all of us in every way that mattered.

To my husband, Nikhil Punde—thank you for always encouraging me to go for it. For cheering on my wild ideas, supporting them without hesitation, and being my quiet partner-in-crime. You've always made space for my dreams.

To Piper and Cooper, my furriest teachers—you've shown me how to stretch my heart wider than I thought possible. You've helped me grow into a gentler, more accepting human. You've taught me what unconditional love really looks like.

To my daughter, Avi—thank you for making me a mother. For helping me experience emotions I never imagined I could hold. You've shown me how to cry tears of joy, laugh without reason, and find magic in the smallest of things. You are the rhythm behind every story in this book.

Thank you, Rupa Shah and Vikas Shah, for proofreading the book and suggesting the edits that I missed. Thank you, Jairaj Vora, for your ongoing support – for cheering on, near or far.

To my team at Voraco, and to all our clients—thank you for holding space for me as I navigated the early days of motherhood, where this book was born. Your patience and support meant more than you'll ever know.

A special thanks to my co-founder, Pramod Maharana, for shouldering so much while I was away.

To Siddhika Narayankar for managing everything with quiet precision so the wheels never stopped turning.

To Nitin Maharana for selflessly helping me put the finishing touches on the design of this book.

A shoutout to Shreekanth Ganesh for bringing soulknit.com to life.

To Jill Sheldekar—thank you for bringing Piper into my life from all the way in Goa. You have been the spark of so many good things in my life.

To ARC Goa—thank you for saving Piper from a terrible fate, believing in her, and caring for her when no one else would. She made it because of you.

To Hemant and Smita Punde—thank you for introducing me to Copper and opening my life to more pets.

To Priya Vadaya—thank you for reminding me to keep telling stories, even when I wasn't sure they were worth telling.

To Anand Ahuja—thank you for pushing me to publish the book. For inspiring me and believing in me. Thank you for all your support.

To all the pets of my childhood—Silky, Brownie, Toffee, and Roi (my first pet—a beta fish). Thank you for shaping me into who I am today. You are still loved. You are the sunshine I borrow on gloomy days.

To my teachers who encouraged me to read, write, and learn, especially to Gayatri Khanna. Thank you for guiding me and engaging me.

To all the friends and family who've published books of your own—you lit the path. Watching you made it seem possible.

A special thank you to Rashi Narang, Founder and CEO of Heads Up For Tails, for answering my cold email and turning it into a beautiful partnership. And to Sakshi Singh Raghuvanshi, Foundation Lead, Heads Up For Tails Foundation, for brainstorming with me, supporting me, and believing in the power of stories.

Thank you to the staff at Blue Tokai for letting me linger with my words and serving me just the right kind of coffee. Thank you for welcoming me, sometimes even before the cafe opened. This book was edited and published in those precious hours I got to myself.

And finally, to the editors, designers, proofreaders, and kind souls who helped in big ways and small—thank you for your generosity. Whether it was reviewing a draft or watching the baby so I could catch my breath, you helped make this possible.

This short book came to life with the help of a long list of people who believed in me and the power of telling stories.

This list now includes *you.*

Thank you for reading the book and making it this far. It is readers like you who inspire the words and the will to write more stories.

With all my love,
Varangi

About the Author

Varangi Vora is an entrepreneur, creative thinker, and lifelong lover of stories—both lived and written. With dual degrees in advertising and visual communication, she has spent over a decade leading global teams. Her work sits at the intersection of strategy and soul, balancing analytical thinking with an eye for nuance.

She lives between cups of coffee, pages of books, and moments of quiet joy with her family—including her husband, daughter, and Piper the cat. When she's not working, writing, or chasing after her toddler, Varangi is most likely immersed in a new creative pursuit or deep into a conversation that meanders just the right amount.

She believes that life is found in the small, ordinary moments—and that telling those stories might just be the most extraordinary thing of all.

www.ingramcontent.com/pod-product-compliance
Ingram Content Group UK Ltd.
Pitfield, Milton Keynes, MK11 3LW, UK
UKHW021400190726
13845UKWH00028B/794

9 789334 397949